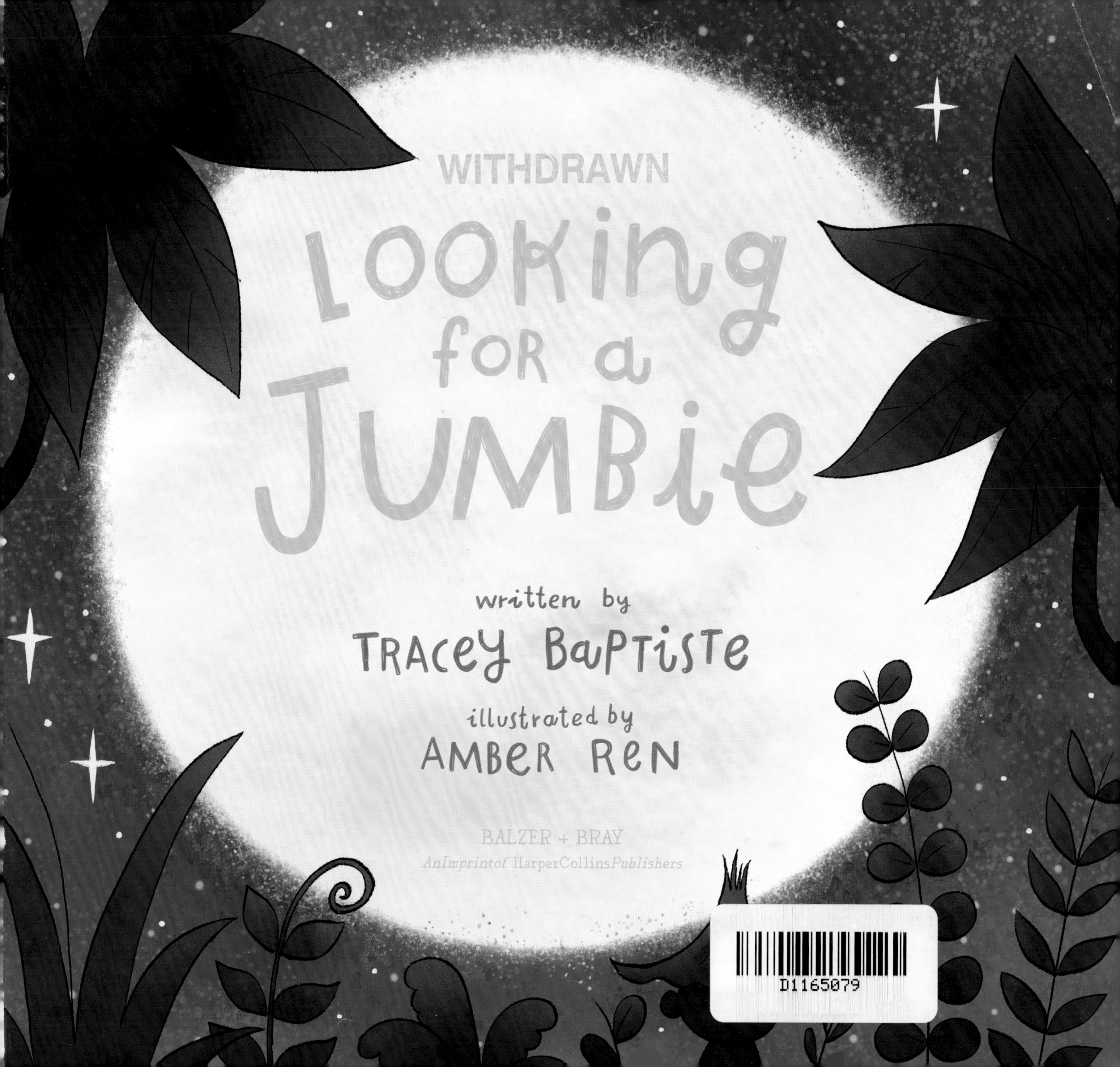
WITHDRAWN
Looking for a Jumbie
written by
Tracey Baptiste
illustrated by
Amber Ren
BALZER + BRAY
An Imprint of HarperCollins Publishers
D1165079

For Nolan and Lucas —T.B.

For my LaoLao, who loved telling me spooky stories that kept me up at night. —A.R.

Balzer + Bray is an imprint of HarperCollins Publishers.

Looking for a Jumbie

Library of Congress Control Number: 2020950511
ISBN 978-0-06-297081-7

The artist used ink and Photoshop to create the digital illustrations for this book.
Typography by Caitlin Stamper
21 22 23 24 25 RTLO 10 9 8 7 6 5 4 3 2 1
❖
First Edition

Reader,

Before you go looking for a jumbie (juhm-bee), you need to know what a jumbie is.

Jumbies are creatures from Caribbean stories. They are like fairies or trolls. And like fairies or trolls, they hide and play tricks on humans. Jumbies are often in scary stories told to frighten kids into staying inside after dark, but jumbies can also be helpful. There are lots of different types of jumbies. Some live in the forest. Some live in the water. Some soar up into the sky.

How about we go find some?

"Come to bed now, Naya," Mama said.
"It's getting dark."

"I'm not scared," Naya said.

"Of what?"

"Jumbies."

"Oh no?" her mama said, laughing. "But they come out at night when the moon is bright to find little ones like you!"

"This moon is perfect for finding jumbies," Naya said.

“This moon is perfect . . . for sleeping! And jumbies are only in stories,” Mama added.

“For true?” Naya said.

“For true,” said Mama.

"I'm looking for a jumbie.

I'm going to find a scary one."

"No such things," whispered a voice from the leaves.

"There are too!" Naya said. "They come out at night when the moon is bright. It's the perfect time to find one."

"What does a jumbie look like?" the voice asked.

"Douen are very small," said Naya, "with backward feet and a great big mouth . . ."

"... like you!"

“Everyone’s mouth is big when they yawn,” said the small someone.

“Well . . . that’s true,” Naya said. “Maybe I should check behind that tree.”

“Good idea!”

“Want to help?” Naya asked.

"We're looking for a jumbie.
We're going to find a scary one."

"A jumbie? Those aren't real!" said a creaky voice in the trees.

"Oh yes, they are!" Naya said. "They come out at night when the moon is bright. It's the perfect time to find one."

"Tell me about them," the voice creaked.

"Lagahoo have thick fur and sharp teeth and chains around their necks . . ."

". . . like you!"

"Well, it's just good sense to wear something shiny when it's dark out," said the tall fellow.

"Maybe you're right," Naya said. "I'm going to try across this field."

"Good idea!"

"Will you come along?" asked Naya.

"We're looking for a jumbie.
We're going to find a scary one."

"I've never heard of those!" sang a sweet voice.
"Well, listen, then!" Naya said. "They come out at night when the moon is bright. It's the perfect time to find one."

"What do they do?" the voice sang.
"Soucouyants fly around in the dark
with skin as bright as flame . . ."

". . . like you!"

"Everyone looks bright in the moonlight," said the woman.

"Hmm . . . I suppose so," Naya said. "I think I'll look over that hill."

"Good idea!"

"Would you like to join us?" Naya asked.

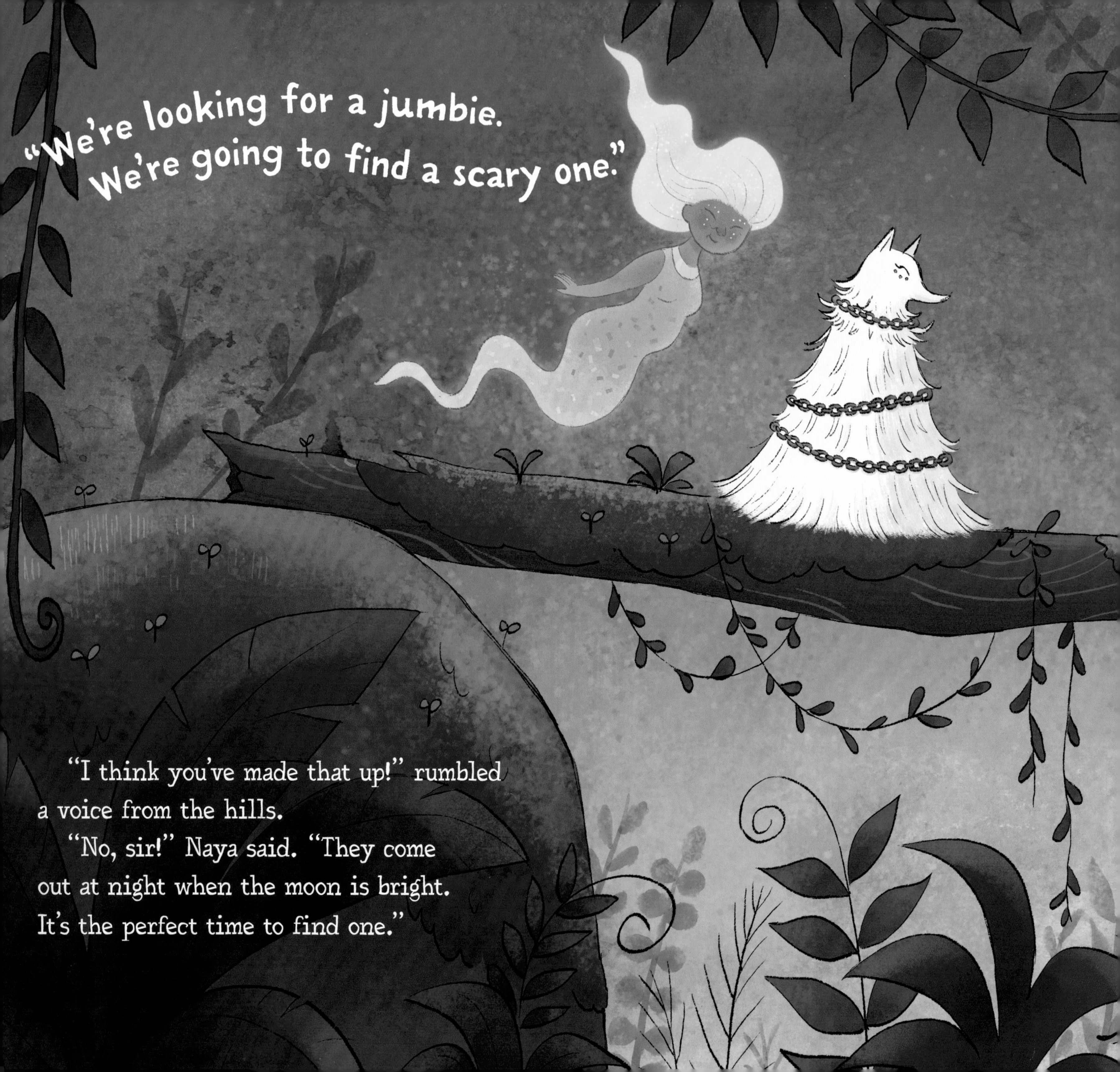

"We're looking for a jumbie.
We're going to find a scary one."

"I think you've made that up!" rumbled a voice from the hills.

"No, sir!" Naya said. "They come out at night when the moon is bright. It's the perfect time to find one."

"How would I know if I saw one?" the voice rumbled.

"Papa Bois has feet like a goat, horns on his head, and tangly hair filled with leaves . . ."

“. . . like you!”

"You'd have messy hair too
if you walked through the bush,"
said their very large friend.

"I guess that's a good point," Naya said.
"How about I check over the river?"

"Good idea!"

"You can come too,"
said Naya.

"We're looking for a jumbie. We're going to find a scary one."

"How will you do that?" said a bubbly voice from the river.

"Don't you know?" asked Naya. "They come out at night when the moon is bright. It's the perfect time to find one."

"What are they like?" the voice asked.

"Mama D'Leau lives in the water and has a long snake tail and pretty coils in her hair . . ."

". . . like you!"

“Thank you. I like your hair too,” said the lady. “I’ll look here. You search that little house.”

“That’s my house, you know,”
Naya said. “Want to see?”

"Mama says jumbies are only in stories," Naya said.

"For true?" the lady said, yawning.

"For true . . ."

". . . but you can't believe
everything you hear in stories."